PUFFIN BOOKS

MUGGIE MAGGIE

Maggie doesn't really mean it when she vows never to join up her writing, but everybody seems to be taking her revolt very, very seriously. Maggie's parents say she'll enjoy it once she starts. Her teacher won't listen when she points out how untidy grown-ups' writing can be. And her class thinks it's hilarious when her first go at signing her name makes it look like 'Muggie'!

Now Maggie is bored with her little rebellion, but she's too proud to back down. If she could only go on printing all her life!

Beverly Cleary is an internationally popular author and her books have earned her many prestigious awards. She was born in Oregon, USA. After graduating from the University of California at Berkeley, she pursued a career as a librarian for many years, before becoming a full-time writer. She is the mother of grown-up twins, and lives with her husband in California.

Muggie Maggie

Beverly Cleary

Illustrated by Anthony Lewis

PUFFIN BOOKS

*To a third-year girl who wondered why no one had
ever written a book to help third years read
joined-up writing*

PUFFIN BOOKS

Published by the Penguin Group
Penguin Books Ltd, 27 Wrights Lane, London W8 5TZ, England
Penguin Books USA Inc., 375 Hudson Street, New York, New York 10014, USA
Penguin Books Australia Ltd, Ringwood, Victoria, Australia
Penguin Books Canada Ltd, 10 Alcorn Avenue, Toronto, Ontario, Canada M4V 3B2
Penguin Books (NZ) Ltd, 182–190 Wairau Road, Auckland 10, New Zealand

Penguin Books Ltd, Registered Offices: Harmondsworth, Middlesex, England

First published by Hamish Hamilton Ltd 1992
Published in Puffin Books 1993
1 3 5 7 9 10 8 6 4 2

Text copyright © Beverly Cleary, 1990
Illustrations copyright © Anthony Lewis, 1992
All rights reserved

The moral right of the author has been asserted

Printed in England by Clays Ltd, St Ives plc
Set in Garamond

Chapter 1

After the first day in her new class, Maggie Schultz
jumped off the school bus when it stopped at her
corner. "Bye, Jo Ann," she called to the girl who
was her best friend, sometimes. "See you tomorrow." Maggie was happy to escape from sixth-year
boys who called her a shrimp and from fourth-year
boys who insisted the third year was awful, joined-
up writing hard, and Mrs Leeper, the teacher,
mean.

Her dog, Kisser, was waiting for her. When Maggie knelt to hug him, Kisser licked her face. He was a young, eager dog the Schultzes had chosen from the Dogs' Home. "A friendly spaniel-cross, looking for a child to love" was the description above his cage, a description that proved to be right.

"Come on, Kisser." Maggie ran home with her fair hair flying and her dog springing along beside her.

When Maggie and Kisser burst through the kitchen door, her mother said, "Hi there, pet. How did things go today?" She held Kisser away from the fridge with her foot while she put away milk cartons and vegetables. Mrs Schultz was good at standing on one foot because five mornings a week she taught exercise classes to overweight women.

"Mrs Leeper is nice, sort of," began Maggie, "except she didn't make me a monitor and she put Jo Ann at a different table."

"Too bad," said Mrs Schultz.

Maggie continued, "Courtney sits on one side

of me and Kelly on the other and that Kirby Jones, who sits across from me, kept pushing the table into my stomach."

"And what did you do?" Mrs Schultz was taking eggs out of a carton and setting them in the white plastic egg tray in the fridge.

"Pushed it back." Maggie thought a moment before she said, "Mrs Leeper said we are going to have a happy year in 3B."

"That's nice." Mrs Schultz smiled as she closed the fridge, but Maggie was doubtful about a teacher who forecast happiness. How did she know? Still, Maggie wanted her teacher to be happy.

"Kisser needs exercise," Mrs Schultz said. "Why don't you take him outside and give him a

workout?" Maggie's mother thought everyone, dogs included, needed exercise.

Maggie enjoyed chasing Kisser around the garden, ducking, dodging, and throwing a dirty tennis ball, wet with dog spit, for him until he collapsed, panting, and she was out of breath from running and laughing.

Refreshed and much more cheerful, Maggie was flipping through television channels with the remote control, trying to find funny commercials, when her father came home from work. "Daddy! Daddy!" she cried, running to meet him. He picked her up, kissed her, and asked, "How's my Goldilocks?" When he set her down, he kissed his wife.

"Tired?" Mrs Schultz asked.

"Traffic gets worse every day," he answered.

"Was it your turn to make the coffee?" demanded Maggie.

"That's right," grumped Mr Schultz, half-pretending.

Other than talking with people who came to see him, Maggie did not really understand what her father did in his office. She did know he made coffee every other day because Ms Madden, his secretary, said she did not go to work in an office to make coffee. He should take his turn. Ms Madden was such an excellent secretary – one who could spell, punctuate, and type – that Mr Schultz put up with his share of coffee-making. Maggie found this so funny that she always asked about the coffee.

"Did Ms Madden send me a present?" Maggie asked. Her father's secretary often sent Maggie a little present: a tiny bottle of shampoo from a hotel, a free sample of perfume, and once, a rubber shaped like a duck. Maggie felt grown-up when she wrote thank-you notes on their home computer.

"Not today." Mr Schultz tousled Maggie's hair and went to change into his jogging clothes.

When dinner was on the table and the family, exercised, happy, and hungry, was seated, Maggie chose the right moment to break her big news. "We start joined-up writing this week," she said with a gusty sigh that was supposed to impress her parents with the hard work that lay ahead.

Instead they laughed. Maggie was annoyed. Joined-up writing was *serious*. She tossed her hair, which was perfect for tossing, waving and curling to her shoulders, the sort of hair that made women say, "What wouldn't you give for hair like that?" or, in sad voices, "I used to have hair that colour."

"Don't look so gloomy," said Maggie's father. "You'll survive."

How did he know? Maggie scowled, still hurting from being laughed at, and said, "Joined-up writing is dumb. It's all wrinkled and stuck together, and I can't see why I am supposed to do it." This was a new thought that popped into her mind that moment.

"Because everyone joins up their writing," said Mrs Schultz. "Or almost everybody."

"But I can write print, or I can use the computer," said Maggie, arguing mostly just to be arguing.

"I'm sure you'll enjoy it once you start," said Mrs Schultz in that brisk, positive way that always made Maggie feel contrary.

I will not enjoy it, thought Maggie, and she said, "All those loops and squiggles. I don't think I'll do it."

"Of course you will," said her father. "That's why you go to school."

This made Maggie even more contrary. "I'm not going to do joined-up writing, and nobody can make me. So there."

"Ho-ho," said her mother so cheerfully that Maggie felt three times as contrary.

Mr Schultz's smile flattened into a straight line. "Just get busy, do what your teacher says, and learn it."

The way her father spoke pushed Maggie further into contrariness. She stabbed her fork into her baked potato so the handle stood up straight, then she broke off a piece of her hamburger with her fingers and fed it to Kisser.

"Maggie, *please*," said her mother. "Your father has had a hard day, and I haven't had such a great day myself." After teaching her exercise classes in the morning, Mrs Schultz spent her afternoons running errands for her family: dry cleaners, bank, petrol station, supermarket, post office.

Maggie pulled her fork out of her baked potato. Kisser licked his chops and looked up at her with hope in his brown eyes, his tail wagging. "Kisser is lucky," she said. "He doesn't have to learn joined-up writing." When her dog heard his name, he stood up and placed his front paws on her lap.

"Now you're being silly, Maggie," said her father. "Down, Kisser, you old nuisance."

Maggie was indignant. "Kisser is not a nuisance. Kisser is a loving dog," she informed her father.

"Don't try to change the subject." Mr Schultz, irritated with Maggie, smiled at his wife, who was pouring him a cup of coffee.

"Books are not written in joined-up writing," Maggie pointed out. "I can read chapter books, and not everyone in my class is good at that."

Mr Schultz sipped his coffee. "True," he admitted, "but many things are handwritten. Memos, many letters, grocery lists, cheques, lots of things."

"I can write letters in printing, and I never write those other things," argued Maggie, "so *I am not going to learn joined-up writing.*" She tossed her hair and asked to be excused.

Kisser felt that he, too, was excused. He trotted after Maggie and jumped up on her bed. As she hugged him, Maggie overheard her mother say, "I don't know what gets into Maggie. Most of the time she behaves herself, and then suddenly she doesn't."

"Contrary kid," said her father.

Chapter 2

The next day, after the 3B monitors had helped with the register, changed the date on the calendar, fed the hamster, and done all the housekeeping chores that monitors have to do in the morning, Mrs Leeper faced her class and said, "Today is going to be a happy day."

3B looked hopeful.

"Today we take a big step in growing up," said Mrs Leeper. "We are going to learn joined-up handwriting. We are going to learn to make our letters flow together." Mrs Leeper made *flow* sound like a long, long word as she waved her hand in a graceful flowing motion.

She calls that exciting, thought Maggie, slumping in her chair.

"How many of you have ridden on a roller-coaster?" asked Mrs Leeper. Half the members of the class raised their hands. Mrs Leeper wrote on the blackboard:

$$a \quad c \quad d \quad m \quad n$$

"Many letters start up slowly, just like a roller-coaster, and then drop down," she said, and she traced over the first stroke of each letter with coloured chalk. Then she went on to demonstrate how the roller-coaster climbed almost straight up:

$$d \quad k \quad h \quad l$$

After the paper monitor passed out paper, the class practised, not whole letters but roller-coaster strokes:

$$r \quad r \quad r \quad /// $$

Maggie did as she was told until she grew bored and began to draw one long roller-coaster line that rose and fell, turned and twisted, and rose again. So many of the class needed help with their strokes that Mrs Leeper did not get around to Maggie.

The next day, after strokes, the class practised whole letters, copying each one several times to make sure it was perfect. This was difficult. 3B frowned, worried, struggled, and asked Mrs Leeper whether they were doing it right. Then they learned to connect letters with straight lines. Maggie went on drawing roller-coasters until Mrs Leeper noticed.

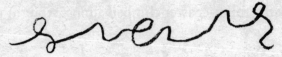

"Why, Maggie," she said, "why haven't you been working on your letters and lines?"

"I am working," said Maggie, "on roller-coasters."

Mrs Leeper looked thoughtfully at Maggie, who tried to look happy. "Roller-coasters are not joined-up writing," said the teacher.

"I know," agreed Maggie, "but I don't need handwriting. I use our computer."

"Maggie, I think you had better stay after school so we can have a little talk," said Mrs Leeper.

"I have to catch my bus," said Maggie with her sweetest smile.

That afternoon, Maggie examined joined-up writing wherever she found it. "Why does your writing on the grocery list lean over backwards?" she asked her mother. "Mrs Leeper says letters should lean forward as if they were walking against the wind."

"I'm left-handed, and my teachers didn't show me how to turn my paper," answered Mrs Schultz.

"And what are those little circles floating around?" asked Maggie.

Her mother laughed. "When I was at junior school, girls often made circles instead of dots over their *i*'s. We thought it was artistic or something. I don't really remember."

That evening, Maggie stood at her father's side as he wrote a letter on the computer. When he pulled the paper out of the printer, he picked up a pen and wrote at the bottom:

"What does that say?" asked Maggie.

"That's how I sign my name," said her father. "Sydney Schultz."

"You didn't add your tails," Maggie pointed out. "You are supposed to add tails to letters that have pieces that hang down." She had learned a thing or two in spite of herself.

"Oops," said Mr Schultz, and he added his tails.

Chapter 3

Maggie began to enjoy handwriting practice. She experimented with letters leaning over backwards and decorated with little circles, the way her mother dotted her *i*'s. She wrote messy *g*'s without their tails, the way her father made his *y*'s.

"Why, Maggie," said Mrs Leeper. "I find your handwriting very untidy."

"I'm writing like a grown-up," Maggie explained.

The result was Mrs Leeper's asking Maggie's mother to come to school for a conference. That day, Mrs Schultz had to fill the petrol tank of the car, go to the bank, buy paper for the computer, and take Kisser to the vet for his injections — all this after teaching exercise classes in the morning.

She was not smiling when she reached school, still wearing her track suit. She handed Kisser's leash to Maggie so she could take care of him during her conference with Mrs Leeper.

Kisser was so happy to see a playground full of children that he wanted to jump up on everyone. Maggie had to hold on to his leash with both hands when her friends gathered round to ask why Mrs Schultz was talking to the teacher.

Jo Ann answered for Maggie. "Maybe Mrs Leeper wants her to be form captain or something."

"I bet," said Kirby on his way to the bus.

"What did she say?" demanded Maggie when her mother returned and everyone had boarded the buses. "What did Mrs Leeper say about me?"

"Down, Kisser!" Mrs Schultz sounded cross. "Mrs Leeper said you are a reluctant joined-up writer who has not reached joined-up writing readiness, and perhaps you are too immature to write it."

Maggie was indignant. "I am not!" she said. "I am Gifted and Talented." Some people were Gifted and Talented, and some people weren't. At least, that was what teachers thought. Maybe no one had told Mrs Leeper how Gifted and Talented she was. Maggie's mother drove home without saying one single word. Maggie hugged Kisser, who was so grateful that he licked her face, which she found comforting. Someone loved her.

For several days, just for fun, Maggie drew fancy letters during handwriting practice, and then Mrs Leeper told her that Mr Galloway, the headteacher, wanted to see her in his office. On her way, Maggie, filled with dread, dawdled as long as she felt she could get away with it.

"Hello there, Maggie," said Mr Galloway. "Sit down and let's have a little talk."

Maggie sat. She never enjoyed what grown-ups called "a little talk".

Mr Galloway smiled, leaned back in his chair, and placed his fingertips together like an *A*, with his thumbs for the crossbar. A printed *A*, of course. "Maggie, Mrs Leeper tells me you are not doing joined-up writing. Can you tell me why?"

Maggie swung her legs, stared at a picture of the Queen on the wall, nibbled a fingernail. Mr Galloway waited. Finally, Maggie had to say something. "I don't want to."

"I see." Mr Galloway spoke as if Maggie had said something very important that required serious thought, lots of it.

"And why don't you want to?" asked the head-teacher after a long silence, during which Maggie studied the way he combed his hair over his bald spot.

"I just don't want to," said Maggie. "I use a computer."

Mr Galloway nodded as if he understood. "That's all, Maggie," he said. "Thank you for coming in."

That evening, Mrs Leeper telephoned Maggie's mother to say that the headteacher had reported Maggie was not motivated to join up her writing. "That means you don't want to," Mrs Schultz explained to Maggie.

"That's what I told him," said Maggie, who couldn't see what all the fuss was about.

"Maggie!" cried her mother. "What are we going to do with you?"

"I'll motivate you, young lady," said Mr Schultz. "No more computer for you. You stay strictly away from it."

Mrs Schultz had more to say. "Tomorrow, Maggie is to see the school psychologist." She looked worried, Mr Schultz looked grim, and Maggie was frightened. A psychologist sounded scary. Kisser understood. He licked Maggie's hand to make her feel better.

As it turned out, Maggie loved the psychologist, who talked in a quiet voice and let her play with some toys while he asked gentle questions about her family, her dog, her teachers – nothing important. He asked about her times tables, and almost as an afterthought, he inquired, "How do you like joined-up writing?"

"OK," answered Maggie, because he was a grown-up.

A couple of days later, Maggie's mother said, "The school psychologist wrote us a letter."

Maggie's feelings were hurt. He had seemed like such a nice man. She had learned to be suspicious of letters from school. This was not the first.

Mrs Schultz continued, "He says it will be interesting to see how long it will take you to decide to write properly."

"Oh," said Maggie.

"How long do you think that will be?" asked Mrs Schultz.

"Maybe for ever," said Maggie, beginning to wish she had never started the whole thing.

Chapter 4

Maggie had grown bored with not doing joined-up writing, but by now the whole of 3B was interested in her revolt. Each day, they watched to see whether she gave in. Her friends talked about it at lunch-time. In the hall, she overheard a fourth year say, "There goes that girl who won't join up her writing." Many people thought she was brave; others thought she was acting stupid. Obviously, Maggie could not back down now. She had to protect her pride.

Courtney and Kelly, best friends who sat opposite one another, did not approve of Maggie.

Courtney said, "Only first and second years print."

Kelly said, "I think you are acting dumb, Maggie."

Jo Ann whispered from the next table, "If you are having trouble, maybe I can help you on Saturday."

"I'm *not* having trouble," Maggie whispered back. "I just don't want to do it." Then she worried. What if others thought Gifted and Talented Maggie couldn't do joined-up writing if she wanted to?

Mrs Leeper handed out individual papers with each person's name, first and last, written in perfect handwriting at the top. "Today we practise our signatures," she said, and she looked at Maggie. "Even if we write letters on computers, we must sign them in our own handwriting."

Maggie studied her neatly written name. If she wrote "Maggie Schultz" and not one letter more, would this be giving in? Not really, she decided, not if she wrote like a grown-up.

While Kirby — a boy who always did what he was told, more or less — gripped his pencil, pressing down so hard he broke the point and had to go to the pencil-sharpener, and Courtney and Kelly wrote with pencils whispering daintily across their papers, Maggie wrote her name the way her father wrote his:

Maggie Schultz

On the next line, she wrote with her left hand, which was difficult:

Kirby worked so hard that he needed a rest. He pushed the table into Maggie's stomach. Maggie pushed it back.

"Mrs Leeper!" said Courtney. "Kirby and Maggie are wrecking our writing."

"They do it all the time," said Kelly.

This brought Mrs Leeper to their table. "See, Mrs Leeper," said Courtney, pointing. "That is where Kirby pushed the table."

"And this is where Maggie pushed it back," said Kelly.

"I'm sure they won't do it again." Mrs Leeper tried to look happy as she paused beside Maggie.

Maggie quickly curved her arm around her paper and bowed her head as if she was working very, very hard.

Mrs Leeper, who often told the class she had eyes in the back of her head, had already seen Maggie's work, if one could really call it work. "Maggie, why are you writing with your left hand when you are right-handed?" she wanted to know.

"That's the way my mother writes," explained Maggie.

Mrs Leeper removed the pencil from Maggie's left hand and placed it in her right. "And where are the tails on your *g*'s that we talked about? Your *l* and *t* are leaning over backwards. We don't want our telephone poles to tip over, do we?"

"I s'pose not," said Maggie.

"Take your paper home and do it again," said Mrs Leeper, "and we must close our *a*. Your name is not Muggie."

Maggie knew she was done for.

"Muggie Maggie," whispered Kirby, as Maggie had expected.

"You keep quiet." Maggie pushed the table into his stomach.

"Mrs Leeper!" cried Courtney and Kelly at the same time.

"I thought we were going to have a happy teacher today," said Mrs Leeper. "Let's be good citizens."

Maggie was sure she would not have a happy breaktime, and she did not. Everyone shouted, "Muggie Maggie! Muggie Maggie!" Kirby started it, of course. He was not a good citizen.

Chapter 5

Later that week, Mr Schultz brought Maggie a present from Ms Madden, a ball-point pen that wrote in either red or blue ink.

"Just what I've always wanted." Maggie was filled with love for Ms Madden, the one grown-up who, Maggie felt, did not pick on her.

"Can I thank her on the computer?" asked Maggie, testing her father.

"You may not. The computer is off limits." Mr Schultz was annoyingly cheerful. "Use your new pen."

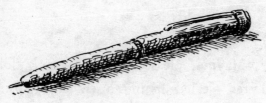

Maggie was not surprised. Her father always meant what he said. She went to her room and, with Kisser resting his nose on her foot, went to work. Her printing was not as neat as it once had been because she was out of practice. She wrote one letter in blue, the next in red, over and over.

Dear Ms Madden,
Thank you for the
pen. I like it.
      Love,
        Maggie

After a moment's thought, she added:

Sorry
So
Sloggy

There. Maggie, pleased with her work, folded the letter, sealed it in an envelope, printed

Ms Madden on the front, and slipped it into her
father's briefcase, with the virtuous feeling of
having done what was expected of her.

The next evening, Mr Schultz brought home an envelope for Maggie, who tore it open. The note, as she had expected, was from Ms Madden and was neatly typed, except for one consonant. It read:

Dear Maggie,
If you are really

$$\left\{ \begin{array}{l} \text{orry} \\ \text{o} \\ \text{loggy} \end{array} \right.$$

(or did you mean sloppy?)
why didn't you copy your
letter out again?
Love,

Hilda Madden

Maggie's eyes filled with tears, she felt so ashamed. Now even Ms Madden, along with everyone else, was picking on her.

Mrs Schultz, seeing Maggie's tears, asked to read the note. Then she said gently, "Well, pet, why didn't you do your letter again?"

Maggie sniffed. "I thought Ms Madden would understand."

Maggie's father took his turn at reading the embarrassing note. "Of course Ms Madden wouldn't understand," he said. "Ms Madden is a secretary who is always neat and accurate."

"Well, I don't want to be a secretary," said Maggie, thinking of several neat, accurate girls in 3B. "I'm going to be an astronaut or a traffic warden."

"Good for you, Goldilocks," said her father, and he rumpled her hair.

Chapter 6

One morning, Maggie noticed Mrs Leeper whispering with other teachers in the hall. They glanced at Maggie, who scrunched down, trying to look invisible so they wouldn't talk about her.

When class started, Mrs Leeper said, "Boys and girls, let's have a happy teacher today." She said that so often, no one paid any attention. Then she pointed to words she had written on the blackboard:

mouth of September

mice day

The words made the class laugh, but Maggie did not see anything funny. Mrs Leeper said, "Maggie, can you tell us what is wrong with these words?"

That was the moment when Maggie discovered she could not read joined-up writing. She shook her head while others, eager to point out the errors, waved their hands.

Later in the day, Mrs Leeper announced, "Class, we need a message monitor. Who wants to be our message monitor?"

Even though she did not expect to be chosen because she was not a person who made Mrs Leeper happy, Maggie raised her hand. So did the rest of the class, except Kirby, who never wanted to be a monitor for anything and who, at the moment, was under the table.

"Maggie, you may be our message monitor," said Mrs Leeper.

"She means Muggie," whispered Kirby, coming up from under the table, where he had been figuring out how the legs were fastened to the top.

"Me?" said Maggie.

"Yes, you," said Mrs Leeper with a happy smile. "And here is a note for you to take to Mr Galloway." She handed Maggie an envelope. "Please wait for an answer."

Maggie lost no time in escaping to the freedom of the hall, where no one supervised her. The envelope was not sealed. Peeking was cheating, Maggie told herself. Bravely and honestly, Maggie carried the note halfway to the headteacher's office. Then she stopped and thought, one peek won't hurt, not if it's quick. If the envelope was not sealed, it must be all right to look inside.

She might have guessed — joined-up writing. Maggie could not figure out the note, which read:

When is this girl ever going
to decide to join up her writing?

Maggie recognized the question mark and decided Mrs Leeper was probably asking for more work sheets or something equally boring.

"Hello there, Maggie," said the headteacher when she held out the note. While Maggie waited, Mr Galloway wrote a short answer, which he put in the same envelope. He crossed out his name and wrote Mrs Leeper's name in its place. The school could not afford to waste envelopes.

"Take this to your teacher," he said with a big smile. "And thank you, Maggie."

I won't look, I won't look, Maggie told herself. What would be the use when the note was hand-written? Maggie walked more and more slowly. Was it wrong to look at something she could not read? Of course not, Maggie decided, and she slipped the note out of the envelope.

Mr Galloway's handwriting was not as neat as Mrs Leeper's, which did not seem right to Maggie. A headteacher's writing should be better than a teacher's.

Maggie will decide to read and write joined-up letters sooner or later. It looks like later.

Maggie studied Mr Galloway's loops and curves until one word jumped out at her: *Maggie*. She was shocked. What was Mr Galloway saying about her? Maggie felt her cheeks turn red. Quickly, she replaced the note and hurried to her classroom as if she was carrying something hot. Mrs Leeper gave her a sharp look and said, "Thank you, Maggie," before she read what the headteacher had written.

Then she smiled, once more a happy teacher.

Suddenly, Maggie found joined-up writing interesting. How could she read people's letters if she could not read handwriting? She couldn't. Maggie, Gifted and Talented Maggie, felt defeat.

Chapter 7

For the next few days Maggie was a busy message monitor because Mrs Leeper sent her hurrying to one room after another. She was even sent to the library. The envelope grew shabby. Most messages contained her name; others did not. Maggie snatched moments in the hall to try to figure out words, but all she learned was that some teachers were careless about joining letters without lifting pencil from paper.

"How come you're delivering so many messages?" asked Kirby.

"Because she can't read joined-up writing," said Courtney.

"And Mrs Leeper knows she can't snoop," said Kelly.

"Mrs Leeper wants me to deliver them," said Maggie. "It makes her happy."

"I bet," said Kirby.

On her way to the infants class, Maggie discovered that all of Mrs Leeper's notes looked exactly alike, which was funny peculiar, not funny ha-ha. Feeling big and important in front of the infants, Maggie wondered about this as she listened to the little children play with the Velcro fasteners on their shoes. *Rip-rip-rip*. This teacher's answer to Mrs Leeper did not contain her name, so Maggie was not much interested. It read:

Keep it up. You will wear
this kid down yet.

In the sixth-year classroom, Maggie felt as if she had shrunk because all the sixth years stared at her while the teacher, a tall man with a

ferocious beard, read the note.

"There's the shrimp," she heard a boy whisper. The class tittered.

The teacher glanced at Maggie, grinned, and wrote a note on the back of an old spelling test. Then he crossed out his name on the ragged envelope, replaced it with Mrs Leeper's name in one of the few spaces left, and handed it to Maggie, who was grateful to escape to the hall.

When she peeked, Maggie found her own name, just as she had in other notes, but this time she found it twice. The note read:

> I once had a bright kid like Maggie who thought she couldn't read joined-up writing — She really could when she tried, but she wouldn't.
> Sounds like Maggie.

Maggie, desperate to read, discovered this teacher was careless about joining letters. If she had time, maybe she could puzzle them out, but she knew that she was expected back in her own classroom. Sending someone to find her would not make Mrs Leeper happy.

Friday evening, Jo Ann telephoned to ask Maggie to spend the night at her house. Maggie said she couldn't. Jo Ann wanted to know why. Maggie said she had to help her father.

"I thought he did some kind of office work," said Jo Ann.

"He does," said Maggie, thinking fast. "I know

how to use our computer." She had not lied, not exactly, but she felt guilty.

That weekend, Maggie studied every bit of handwriting she could find: her mother's tipping-over-backwards grocery list, Ms Madden's neat handwritten notes mixed in with papers her father brought home from the office, anything. She did not try to read her father's writing. She knew it was hopeless.

Maggie spent most of her time in her room with her door closed. With Kisser's nose resting on her foot and some old work papers in front of her, she frantically practised joining up letters, including the difficult ones: *k f r*

"What are you doing, Maggie?" asked her mother through the door.

"Nothing," answered Maggie, aware that her mother felt children were entitled to privacy and would not open the door. Letting her parents know she had changed her mind would make Maggie feel ashamed, like admitting she had been wrong.

Maggie worked hard, and by Sunday evening she agreed with what Mrs Leeper had been saying all along: many joined-up letters are shaped like printed letters. She knew she could read handwriting as long as it was neat. She practised her signature with her letters leaning into the wind:

Maggie Schultz Maggie Schultz

When she had finished, Maggie's face was flushed, her hair more tousled than usual, but she could do joined-up writing. Maybe it wasn't perfect, but anyone past the second year could read it. She went to her father, who was working at the computer. "Daddy, listen to me," she said, and her voice was stern.

Mr Schultz turned from the keyboard. "OK, Maggie, what's up?"

"In writing, neatness counts," Maggie informed him.

"I expect it does," he agreed.

"Then you should learn to add your tails and put the right number of peaks on your *u*'s and write neatly," said Maggie.

"Funny, Ms Madden says the same thing," said Mr Schultz. "I'll try. Cross my heart."

Maggie was not sure she believed him. Next, Maggie went to her mother and announced, "You should make your writing lean the other way like it's supposed to and stop putting silly circles over your *i*'s."

Mrs Schultz smiled and pushed Maggie's hair back from her flushed face. "I don't know about that, pet," she said. "Everyone says my handwriting is distinguished."

Maggie was tired and cross. "Well, it's wrong," she said, and she sighed so hard that Kisser looked anxious. Grown-ups were so hard to reform – maybe impossible.

Chapter 8

On Monday, Maggie looked at the words Mrs Leeper had written on the blackboard and discovered she was reading them because *she couldn't help it*. Mrs Leeper had written:

This is going to be a happy week. We are going on a field trip.

Maggie was eager to carry the next message. She did not have to wait long for Mrs Leeper to write a note for the headteacher. As soon as she closed the door – quietly, no slamming – Maggie slipped out the note that was written on the back of an old arithmetic paper and read the neatly formed words:

Maggie is now reading joined-up writing. I saw her reading what I had written on the blackboard.
If she can read it, she can write it. She just won't admit it.

Maggie was shocked. Maggie was angry. Mrs Leeper had guessed she would peek. Maybe she had guessed all along, and now that Maggie could read joined-up writing, she was saying mean things about her. But worst of all, Mrs Leeper was waiting for an answer.

Maggie wanted to crumple the note, but if she did that, Mrs Leeper would want to know why Mr Galloway had not sent a reply. She returned the note to its tattered envelope, dragged her feet into the headteacher's office, and thrust it at him. She stood staring at the floor while he read it.

"Um-hm," he murmured, and Maggie heard his pen move across paper. "There you go, Maggie," he said as he handed the remains of the envelope back to her. "Thank you."

"You're welcome," said Maggie, and she got out of his office as fast as she could without running.

I won't peek, I won't peek, she told herself, but of course, she finally had to peek. What normal third year wouldn't want to know what the headteacher had to say in time of crisis? This note said:

Hooray! I can tell by the way she behaves that you are right. Good teaching, Laura! I knew you could do it.

Congratulations, Maggie!

Figuring out the long word before her name took a while, and then – well! First of all, Maggie was astonished that Mr Galloway would call a teacher by her first name. Then Maggie was indignant. Mrs Leeper hadn't done a thing. Maggie had done all the work, and now her teacher was getting all the credit.

Maggie dreaded returning to her classroom. She plodded along, trying to figure out how she could avoid it. She couldn't, not even if she took time to go to the bathroom. Sooner or later she had to face her teacher.

With red cheeks, she handed her teacher the remains of the envelope and was about to hurry to her seat when Mrs Leeper caught her hand, pulled Maggie to her, gave her a big hug, and said, "I don't think we need a message monitor any more.

Anyway, the envelope is worn out." She tossed it, along with the note, into the wastebasket and said, "This is a happy day, Maggie."

Maggie was both pleased and confused. She had expected Mrs Leeper to say something about joined-up writing, but the teacher had not. She had not even said, "It's about time," or "I knew you could do it." She just smiled at Maggie, who finally felt she could smile back.

"You know something, Mrs Leeper?" Maggie said shyly. "Your writing is neater than any other teacher's."

Mrs Leeper laughed. "It has to be. I'm the one who teaches it."

Maggie walked slowly to her seat. She could now make her letters flow together, and she had made her teacher happy, but maybe when she grew up and did not have to please grown-ups all the time, she might decide not to write joined-up. She could print any time she wanted. She had plenty of time to think it over.

"Muggie Maggie," said Kirby. "Teacher's pet."

Maggie decided against pushing the table into his stomach.

Instead, she sat down and wrote a note in joined-up writing, which she shoved across the table:

You stop pushing the table into my stomick.

Sinceerly,
Maggie

Also in Young Puffin

Mouldy's Orphan

Gillian Avery

**Mouldy dreams how lovely it would be
if she could adopt a poor orphan and
keep him warm and happy ever after.**

But when she finally finds one and brings
him home to their crowded cottage, Mum
and Dad aren't pleased at all.

Also in Young Puffin

Dinner Ladies Don't Count

Bernard Ashley

Two children, two problems and trouble at school.

Jason storms around the school in a temper – and then gets the blame for something he didn't do. Linda tells a lie, just a little one – and is horrified to see how big it grows. Just as it seems that things can't possibly get worse, help comes for both of them in surprising ways.

Also in Young Puffin

NO HOLIDAY FUN FOR SAM

Thelma Lambert

Will Sam have any fun on holiday?

When Sam sees the words NO BUCKETS AND SPADES IN THE HOUSE in his hotel, he knows he's in for a dismal holiday. Kippers for breakfast and pouring rain...will he ever survive it? Adding to that, Sam's cub pack plan to go camping in Wales. Sam is really excited at the idea, but well-laid plans can go wrong...

Also in Young Puffin

DUSTBIN CHARLIE

Ann Pilling

"Is a skip bigger than a dustbin?"
"*Much* bigger."
"Well, they're getting one for
Number 10."

Charlie had always liked seeing what
people threw out in their dustbins. So
he's thrilled to find the toy of his dreams
among the rubbish in the skip. But
during the night, someone else takes it.

Also in Young Puffin

I'm Trying to Tell You

Bernard Ashley

If you had a chance to talk about your school, what would you say...honestly?

Nerissa, Ray, Lyn and Prakash are all in the same class at Saffin Street School. Each of them has a story to tell about their school – sometimes dramatic, sometimes quiet, but always with a real sense of humour.

THE DEAD LETTER BOX

Jan Mark

"I've got to see you," Louie said. "I've had this terrific idea."

Louie got the idea from an old film which showed how spies left their letters in a secret place – a dead letter box.
It was just the kind of thing that she and Glenda needed to help them keep in touch. And she knew the perfect place for it!

ENOUGH IS ENOUGH

Margaret Nash

"Now enough is enough, Class 1."

Usually when Miss Boswell uses her magic phrase, it works: Class 1 knows that she means enough is *enough*, and gets back to work. But when Miss Boswell's special plant begins to grow and grow until it has wiped the sums off the board and curled right out of the classroom, not even shouting "Enough is enough" will stop it!

Also in Young Puffin

CHRIS
and the
DRAGON

Fay Sampson

Chris Chudley is never out of trouble!

Chris just can't help getting into mischief
– even when he decides to try extra hard
to be good! Starting with an exploding
dragon in a Christmas display and ending
with another kind of dragon – Mrs
Maltby the headmistress! – Chris's
exploits around town and at school make
hilarious reading.

Also in Young Puffin

No Prize or Presents for Sam

Thelma Lambert

Sam has always wanted a pet of his own.

Sam sets out to get himself a pet to enter in the Most Unusual Pets Competition at the village fête. But the animal he chooses leads to some very unexpected publicity.

Sam decides it is up to him to give his Aunty and Uncle a happy Christmas when his Aunty loses her job. But how can he earn some money?

Also in Young Puffin

Anna, Grandpa, and the Big Storm

Carla Stevens

"Do you think I've never seen snow
before?" asked Grandpa. "Anna's
going to school, and I'm going to take
her. And that's that!"

Anna is determined to get to school for
the final of the spelling competition. But
as she and her Grandpa struggle through
the blizzard, Anna wonders if they will
ever get there and, when their train gets
stuck, if they will ever get home again!

Also in Young Puffin

THE SPY
BEFORE YESTERDAY

Catherine Storr

"My dad was a spy . . ."

And so begins the story of Ben's dad's
past. Ben feels he is surrounded
by interesting friends. But Ben is just
Ben, and his dad is ordinary Old Harris,
the Head and maths teacher. But has his
dad ever been anything more? What he
might have been and done develops in
Ben's mind until he finds himself in an
extraordinary amount of trouble!

The Twig Thing

Jan Mark

As soon as Rosie and Ella saw the house they knew that something was missing.

It has lots of windows and stairs, but where is the garden? After they move in, Rosie finds a twig thing which she puts in water on the window-sill. Gradually things begin to change.

Tales of Polly and the Hungry Wolf

Catherine Storr

The wolf is no match for clever Polly!

The wolf is up to his old habit of trying
to trick Polly so that he can gobble her
up. He has thought of several new ways
of getting her into his clutches but Polly
is too clever to allow herself to be caught
by a stupid wolf and she outwits him at
every turn!